Spy Not

TITLE III

by PJ Gray

SADDLEBACK
EDUCATIONAL PUBLISHING
www.sdlback.com

All source images from Shutterstock.com

ISBN-13: 978-1-68021-131-3
ISBN-10: 1-68021-131-5
eBook: 978-1-63078-464-5

Printed in the U.S.A.

20 19 18 17 16   1 2 3 4 5

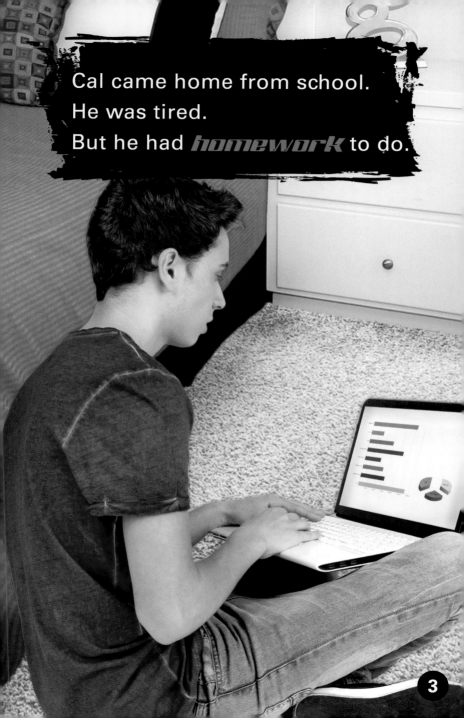

Cal came home from school.
He was tired.
But he had *homework* to do.

3

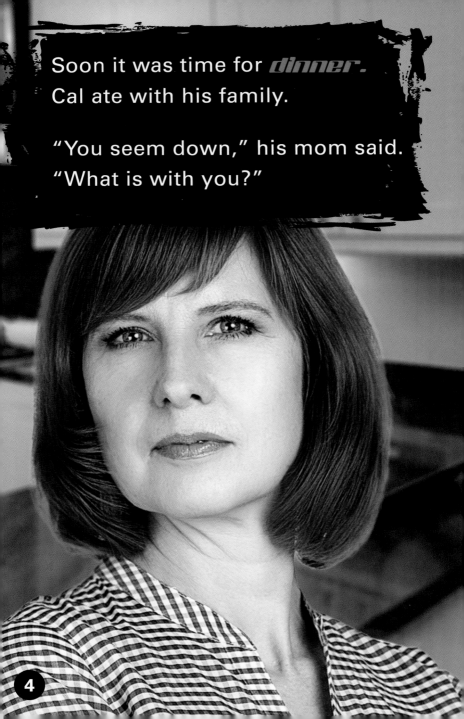

Soon it was time for *dinner.*
Cal ate with his family.

"You seem down," his mom said.
"What is with you?"

Cal picked at his food. "I'm okay," he said.

"Your birthday is next week," his mom said.

"So what?" Cal said.

"You don't want your *birthday?*"

"I don't care," he said.

Ann was Cal's sister. She rolled her eyes.

Cal went to his room after dinner.
His dad came to see him.
He held out a box.
"This is for you," his dad said.

"What is this?" Cal asked.

"It's for your birthday. It's your
gift. We want you to have it now."

Cal opened the box.
"Wow!" he said. "It's what
I wanted!"

9

It was a *drone.*
Cal was happy.

His dad smiled.
"Have fun," he said. "But be careful. A drone is not a toy. You are older now. You have to think about other people."

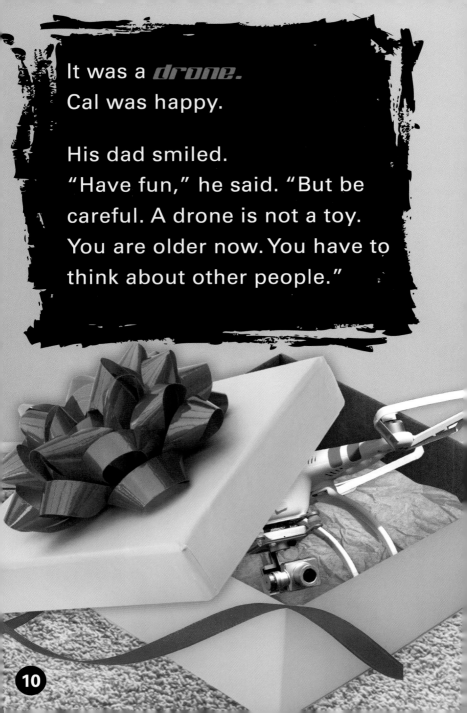

"I'm not a kid," Cal said.

"I know," his dad said. "Just think of others. Drones can scare people."

"I'll be careful," Cal said. "Thanks, Dad."

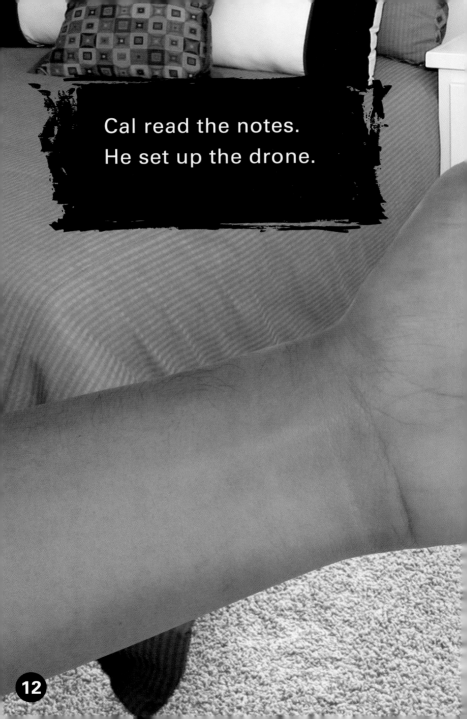

Cal read the notes.
He set up the drone.

He used his phone to fly it.
It was *fun.*

The drone had a *camera* in it.
The camera filmed things.
Cal could see it all on his phone.

14

Cal tested the drone.
He sent it to his desk.
Then he sent it to his window.
It flew around the room.

The next day came.
Cal was home from school.

His mom was on her cell.
Cal walked by.
She turned away.
She talked into the cell.
"I can't talk now.
I have to go."

Cal smiled. "Who was that?"

"Nobody," his mom said.
"Do you want a snack?"

Cal felt odd.
What was she *hiding?*

A few more days went by.
Ann's room was across from Cal's.
He walked past her door.

He saw Ann's friend. It was Tori.
Cal liked Tori. She was *cute.*

Ann spoke softly to Tori.
"You can't tell anyone."

"I won't," Tori said.

Cal walked into Ann's room.
"Hi," Cal said to Tori. "What's up?"

Ann was mad.
"Get out!" she yelled.
"Get out of my room!"

Ann jumped off the bed.
She ran over to Cal.
Then she pushed him away.
"Mom!" Ann yelled. "Tell Cal to leave us alone!"

She slammed the door.

Cal's face was red.
What did Tori think?
Now Cal was mad too.

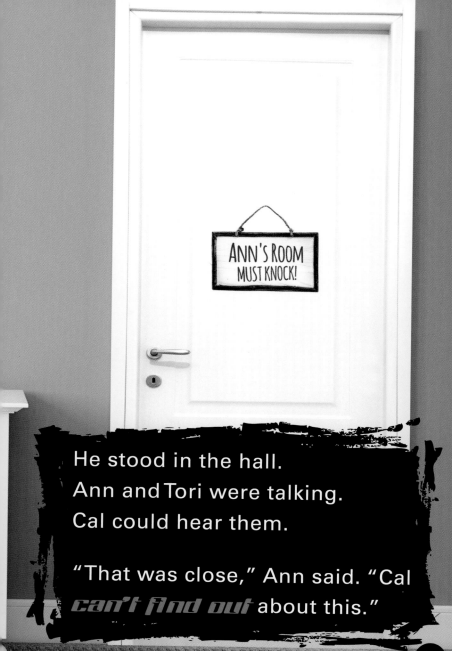

ANN'S ROOM
MUST KNOCK!

He stood in the hall.
Ann and Tori were talking.
Cal could hear them.

"That was close," Ann said. "Cal *can't find out* about this."

Cal had a *plan.*
He ran to his room.
His drone was there.

He opened the window.
Then he used his phone.
The drone took off.
It flew out the window.

The drone went to Ann's window.
Cal ran back by her door.
He looked at his phone.

The camera worked!
Ann's bedroom was on his screen.
His sister was using her *laptop.*

The girls were talking.
Cal heard Ann.
"It's Friday night," she said.

"This party will be fun," Tori said.
"What about your mom and
dad?"

"They won't find out," Ann said.

Cal smiled.
Ann was going to a party.
It was a secret. Now Cal knew it.
He was going to *bust her!*

Friday night came.
Cal was in his room.
Ann was at the front door.
He could hear her.

"I'm going to Tori's house," she said.

"Okay," their mom said. "Dad and I are going to a *movie.*"

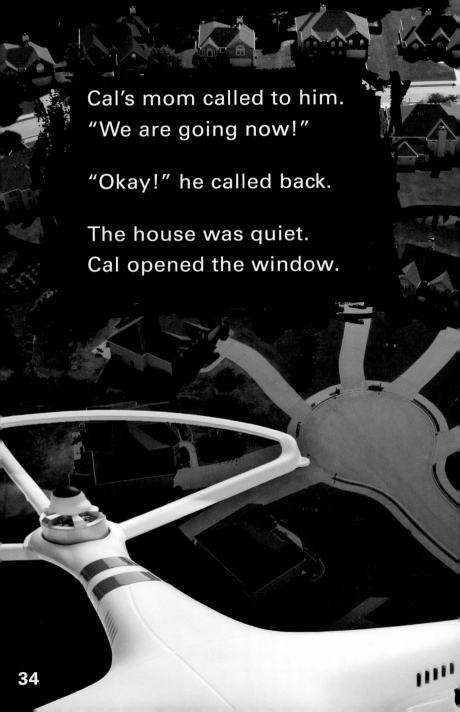

Cal's mom called to him.
"We are going now!"

"Okay!" he called back.

The house was quiet.
Cal opened the window.

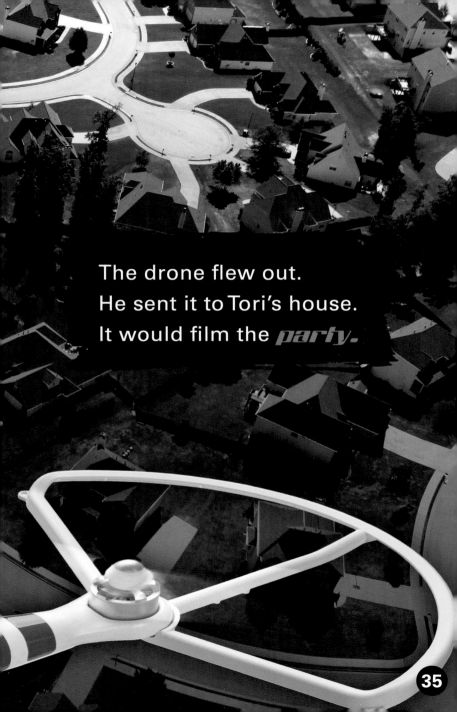

The drone flew out.
He sent it to Tori's house.
It would film the *party.*

Cal watched from his phone.
The drone flew down the street.
He saw the houses.
The trees. The cars.
Tori's house was near.

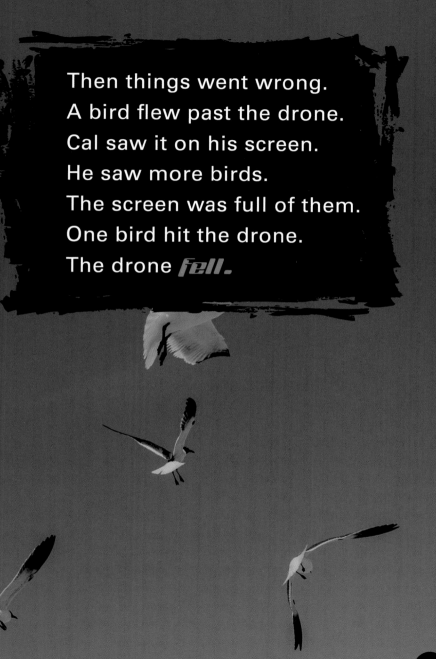

Then things went wrong.
A bird flew past the drone.
Cal saw it on his screen.
He saw more birds.
The screen was full of them.
One bird hit the drone.
The drone *fell.*

Cal was mad.
He tapped on his phone.
He tried to start the drone.
But it did not work.
The drone would not fly.
He had to get it.

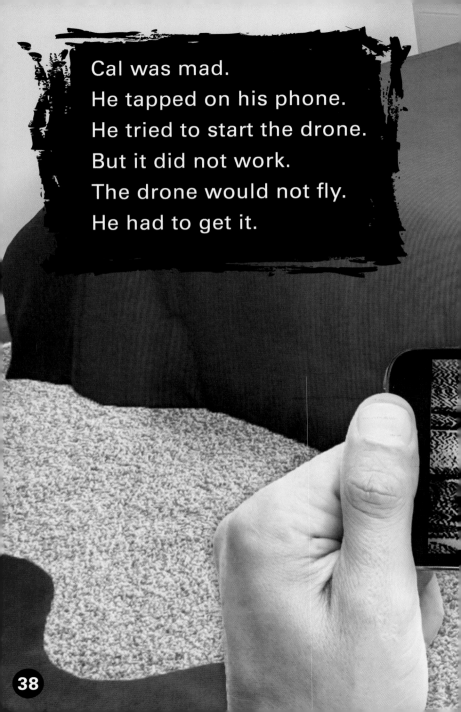

Cal ran out of his house.
He ran to Tori's front yard.
There was *music.*
It was from inside the house.
The party had started!

Cal looked for the drone.
He saw it on the grass.
It was broken.
His gift was *ruined.*

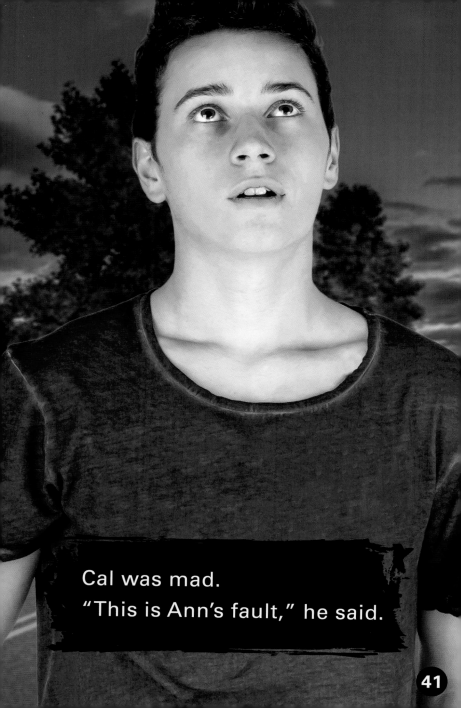

Cal was mad.

"This is Ann's fault," he said.

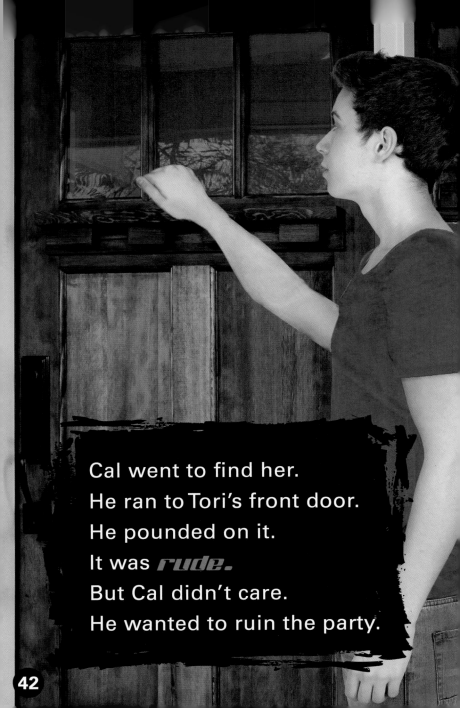

Cal went to find her.
He ran to Tori's front door.
He pounded on it.
It was *rude.*
But Cal didn't care.
He wanted to ruin the party.

Tori opened the door.
She smiled.
"Come in, Cal," she said.

He saw a lot of people.
"Happy birthday!"
they called out.

Cal saw his mom and dad.
He saw Ann.
All of his friends were there.

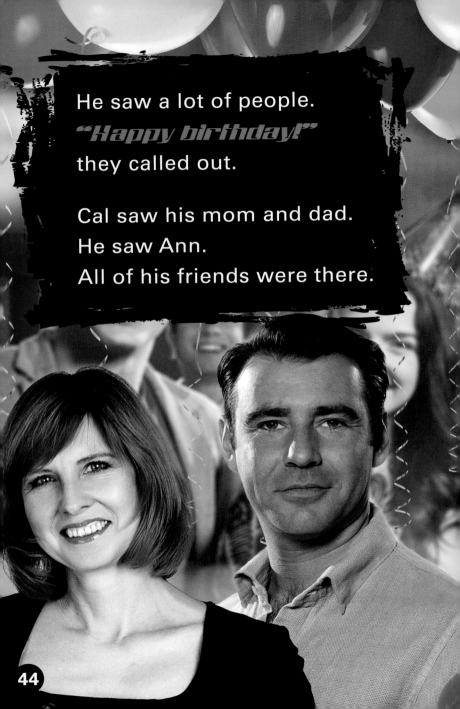

"What?" Cal said. "What is this?"

"It's your birthday party," Ann said.

Cal shook his head.
He looked at Ann.
"But this was your party. It was a secret. I heard you say so."

Ann and Tori laughed.

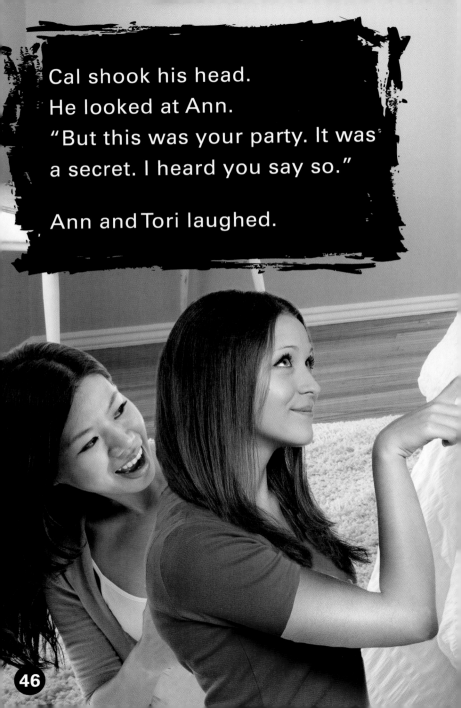

"That was a lie," Ann said. "We saw your drone out my window."

49

TEEN EMERGENT READER LIBRARIES

BOOSTERS

The Literacy Revolution Continues with New TERL Booster Titles!

Each Sold Individually

EMERGE [1]

9781680211139

9781680211528

9781680211153

9781680211153

9781680211122